Perfect Crime
Episode 3
The End of Horror

RICHARD J. GARCIA

CONTENTS

CHAPTER 1

There's always a reason, Daisy told herself. First, Freddie
and Katie divorced, and it had to be while she was with child.
There's got to be a reason. Did Katie change her mind?

It had been a crazy three months and she still couldn't
understand what had happened. Right now, she was on her
way to meet Freddie.

She checked the digital clock on her car and noted that
there's still thirty minutes before their agreed upon time.
She didn't want to keep Freddie waiting.

The sky was dark and there were no stars above; and it
reminded her of a particular night in the past—one that
ended with Michael's demise. Was it her fault that she
wanted to be happy and that Michael was a hindrance to
that? Daisy opened the windows of the car, and her neatly
arranged hair was blown. She had no option then but to

remove the pins on her hair, and let the wind blow her blonde curls. She felt free.

At exactly eight in the evening, she arrived at the restaurant and was looking for a parking spot. She changed her mind and looked for valet instead. When she alighted the car, the maitre d' was waiting for her as though he knew of her arrival. She was led to a table that was inside a private dining area. The lights were warm, and there were no other guests there but her.

She checked her gold watch and saw that it had been ten minutes after eight, and Freddie had not arrived yet. She sat down on the chair that was facing the doorway.

"Would you like to see the menu?" the waiter asked.

Daisy said no and just sat waiting.

Her thoughts were flying. What would happen to Katie now?

She heard a noise from the door and her gaze fell upon the restaurant's entrance where two people could be seen.

The first was Freddie, tall and lean, but with broad shoulders. The second was— to her surprise— Katie!

Blood drained from Daisy's face when they both turned at the same time.

Daisy couldn't believe what she saw. They were approaching

her. Freddie was smiling, but Katie's face was blank. Daisy's heart started to pound.

Katie reached the table first.

"Hi," she said. Her stomach already showed the bulge since she has been with child for five months already.

"Hello," Daisy said. Before she could say anything else, Freddie had taken a chair, pulled it and asked Katie to sit down.

Then Freddie moved closer to Daisy and sat beside her.

He clasped her hand and looked at her intently.

"Don't be surprised," Freddie said. "I took the time to invite her over. The baby will be out in a few months, and I can't totally exclude Katie from my life now that she's carrying our child."

"Of course," Daisy said. Her face was still pale.

Katie was there just staring at Daisy. When Daisy met her stare, Katie smiled and Daisy was able to breathe in relief.

"I don't know if I should apologize," Daisy began. "About what happened between you and Freddie—"

"It's okay," Katie said immediately. "I know it is surreal. But Freddie and I know that our marriage was going to be," she paused, "challenged."

Freddie nodded. "We both decided on the divorce. I don't want your friendship to break. That is why I invited Katie to join us. I hope you understand how my life will always be intertwined with hers." At that last note, Freddie's voice softened as though he was seeking understanding.

Daisy caught Katie's eyes. The other woman was misty eyed that Daisy felt her heart glow. She removed her hands from Freddie's grip and she reached out to hold Katie's hands.

"I am so sorry," Daisy said. "This isn't what I would prefer. But—"

"It's okay," Katie said. Tears had started to flow from the corner of her eyes. "I forgive you. Both of you. And I choose to be happy alone rather than to remain married to someone who's seeing someone else."

Katie turned to look at Freddie and continued speaking as though what she was about to say was with his approval.

"I am here because—" Katie paused. She took something from her purse. It was a small black box.

Daisy's breath caught as she glimpsed the box.

Katie opened it and inside was a diamond ring.

"What are you doing?" Daisy said.

Katie laughed weakly, and there was affection when she continued to speak. "To show you that I harbor no bad feelings towards you and Freddie, I am here with Freddie," she paused and turned to look at Freddie who had actually stood up and knelt down as though on cue. He was looking at Daisy.

"I am here with Freddie," Katie repeated, "to ask your hand in marriage on his behalf. Daisy, will you be Freddie's wife?"

Daisy's eyes widened in surprise. She put a hand over her already opened mouth and gasped.

"This is unheard of! Oh my god! Are you two serious?" she said.

"As certain as I ever could become," Freddie said.

Daisy looked at Freddie and then at Katie. Then back to Freddie again. When she still did not answer, Freddie stood up.

"I want to marry you. Please do me the honor of being your husband," he said.

Daisy blushed furiously, and when she saw how sincere the two looked, she finally found the courage to speak.

"There's nothing I want more than to marry you, she said while quickly darting a glance towards Katie.

Freddie beamed and took it as his cue. He got the diamond ring and placed it on Daisy's ring finger.

It sparkled as light touched the diamond. This time, it was Daisy's eyes that became misty.

Then as though to break whatever tension that surrounded them, they all laughed. The laughter was weak until as seconds passed by, the laughter became hearty, and no one— not a single soul who could have been witnessing what was happening could contest that it was the most beautiful thing they've seen.

Freddie moved and sat beside Daisy. He cupped her face and kissed her lightly on the lips.

"To our forever," he said.

"To ours," Daisy repeated.

In two weeks, Freddie and Daisy were married. The wedding ceremony was simple, not the ostentatious one that Daisy thought one would have between two rich people.

CHAPTER 2

Freddie spent most of his days living in Daisy's home. Katie had told him that Daisy had money, and yet, he couldn't believe that the house that they were living in was just a simple bungalow in Canada.

He had agreed to move in with her. The good thing about it was that Katie agreed to move to Canada too. That way when she gives birth in a few months, he would be there to support her.

If Daisy had the money the way Katie had said, why was there no household help? He frowned as he watched the dirty dishes pile up on the kitchen sink.

"Daisy," he said. "Everything's a mess here. Will you please tidy up?"

Freddie's family had money that's why he grew up not being accustomed to doing household chores.

Daisy came rushing in. "I just had my nails done," she said.

"But all you have to do is put everything in the dishwasher—"

Freddie said.

Daisy sensed her husband's disapproval so she tiptoed to kiss him lightly and then she moved to clean up.

There was no urgency in her movements as though she had all the time in the world.

Frustrated, Freddie went outside and lit a cigarette.

After the marriage, he noticed that there were a lot of changes to how Daisy behaved. There were little quirks that he didn't notice before.

At times, Daisy would coldly push him away in bed. Which as far as he could recall never happened when they were still dating.

Most of the time, Daisy would go out alone. Either to meet a friend— or friends— none of whom were ever introduced to him. He knew that it was wrong to feel the way he did, to be doubting his wife, and yet he was almost certain that the moment they gave their vows, a connection between them had snapped.

He took out his mobile phone and paused for a moment, wondering if he should call Katie, his ex-wife.

"Hello," he said over the phone when finally he decided to call her.

"Hi there, soon to be father," the sweet voice of Katie said.

He couldn't help it, he smiled. In his head he was wondering if his agreement to the divorce was right. What if he made the wrong decision. It was all for the money, Katie had told him. And yet, he still had not glimpsed of her riches. He wanted to talk about it to Katie, but he decided otherwise.

"Did you go see your gynecologist?" He asked.

Katie laughed. "Why the hell do you want to know?"

"I'm concerned about the baby," he said.

Katie laughed even louder. "I don't think so," she said cheerily. I know you enough to say that you don't usually bother with things like small talks."

Freddie chortled. "You got me there."

"Of course I know you," she said. "I spent a year with you!" She finished as though it was obviously the reason she came to that conclusion.

"Well—," he said. He laughed weakly. "Why did I ever agree to divorce you?" He said.

It was Katie's turn to chortle. "Um, one word—money."

Freddie nodded to himself. Should he tell Katie about his doubts on Daisy's actual financial condition, but decided not to for the second time that day.

Instead of telling her about it, he simply changed the topic and told her about how his day at work was. He barely noticed that inside the kitchen, Daisy had already finished cleaning up, that she was now on the porch watching him as he flirted on the phone with his ex-wife. Nor was he oblivious to the fact that instead of Daisy becoming surly over his actions, she was actually smiling as she turned around and walked back inside the house.

CHAPTER 3

It had been months now since the divorce. There were times that Katie missed Freddie, if only for the company he used to afford her, and for his silly jokes. Yet divorcing him was all part of the plan and she could not be regretful about it.

She was lying in bed, holding her bulging stomach and wondering when the baby would come out.

It would be a boy, the gynecologist had told her. She couldn't believe it! A baby boy. How lucky could one get?

Since she could dream of having a child, it had always been a boy that she wanted. Everything— all the things that she planned on would culminate to living luxuriously with her child. And now, that is close to happening.

She wanted the baby to be born already. But was one child enough?

She wanted another child. And she didn't like the notion of having two kids from different men. So how would she do it.

It had been a careful study of a man's character that she succumbed to. All her life, she knew that men were easy to tempt and her ex-husband was one like that. He was an easy prey to her plans.

She touched her belly gently, lovingly. And with the lights on, she fell asleep soundly that night.

***

Her phone was ringing and she woke up with her hands moving to pick up the phone as though it had its own life.

"Hello," she said.

It was a woman on the other end of the line.

"I miss you," the other person said.

She wondered inside her head if she should respond. Would it be dangerous to say the same over the phone? She maintained her ground and decided that since her plans were about to come to a culmination, it was better to stay safe than sorry.

So even with a heavy heart, she decided to put the phone down.

***

The next day, she was awoken from sleep by the tightening in her belly. The baby was kicking her. Her lower back ached. When she stood up, water grazed her legs. When realization struck her about what was happening, she immediately took her phone and called Freddie.

"We're having a baby!" she shouted. Then she put the phone down and went to get her utility bag.

When she went outside, she was already having difficulty walking. Her body was hurting all over and all she wanted was to sit down.

Loud screeching of car's wheels followed and she sighed in relief as she saw Freddie's car approaching the driveway. It halted and from the passenger side, Daisy came out. She grabbed the bag that Daisy was holding and escorted her to the backseat. She settled uncomfortably.

"We 'll be there soon," Freddie said.

Katie wanted to be thankful that Daisy was with them, sitting next to her, but the pain on her belly, her lower back, had prevented her from smiling.

Instead of being grateful to both of them, she shrieked, "Hurry up!"

Freddie hit the gas pedal and in a few minutes, they arrived at the hospital.

At the braking of dawn, Dominic was born.

When Katie was holding the baby in her arms, she knew that everything she had ever done in her life was worth it. She now had a child.

CHAPTER 4

"Where are you going?" Daisy asked Freddie.

"Katie needs something from the grocery. She asked me if I can pick up a few things for my son," he said.

Daisy frowned. Lately that had always been the case.

At first, it was okay with her—Freddie running an errand for the baby— but lately, Daisy was not sure anymore if he was making an excuse. Did he really have to get something for the baby or was he just looking for a way to get out of the house and away from her?

"There are stuff I need you to help me on too," she said.

"Like pay the bills for the house rent because you forgot to withdraw yesterday?" Freddie said with a hint of sarcasm.

"That's not a very nice thing to say. I'm your wife. We're supposed to shoulder the expenses together," she said sternly.

Freddie looked to be ashamed of what he said. Under the heat of the sun, he blushed. "I'm sorry," he said. Then he walked towards Daisy and held her. "It's really just the baby. I want a baby— and besides, the baby I will be visiting is my own."

That was another thing. Daisy's stomach turned sour as she remembered her attempts to have a child of her own. Back when she was so much younger she had been reckless, and there were instances that she had one night stands with people she met in the bars. It was back when she was still having an identity crisis, back when she was striving to be straight. And yet the years told her otherwise as girl friends came and went into her life. That was why up until now— six months after her marriage to Freddie— she still sometimes wonder if she made the right decision. The doubts had started growing inside her head most especially now that Freddie had been acting weirdly. And then there were times that Katie acted as though she had a plan. She used to be part of that plan— but when Katie married Freddie in the past, Daisy had felt betrayed and was left out wondering what had happened. The divorce was even more puzzling.

She didn't seem to understand her friend anymore.

Daisy watched as Freddie left.

"Will you be back for dinner?" Daisy shouted so Freddie could still hear her, but there was a good hundred yards separating them already. If ever Freddie heard her, she wasn't sure anymore because he didn't reply to her question.

* * *

Daisy had not been a fan of the movies, but she decided to go. She was smiling as she went out of the movie house and felt lighter. The romantic comedy that she watched was such a delight. Since she wasn't sure what time Freddie would be back, she checked the next movie schedule. There was a good listing of suspense thriller movies, and she became nostalgic as she remembered that Katie and she used to go to movies together to catch the latest non stopping, breath taking film. And now she's all alone to do it.

After purchasing another ticket, she bought popcorn and soda and went inside another cinema.

Inside, she felt uneasy. Why wasn't Freddie calling her? Or at least send her a text message to let her know where he was already? She was looking at the blank screen of the phone, frowning, her heart confused and hurt when her phone's screen began flashing.

Katie was calling her.

"Hello," she said. It felt good and ironic at the same time to hear her voice.

"Where are you?" Katie asked.

"Um, at the mall. "

"Listen, I need to see you," Katie said.

"But what about the baby," Daisy said. She knew that Katie doesn't have a nanny for young Dominic.

"I will leave him with Freddie," Katie said.

Daisy's heart plummeted. "Oh, so he is still there?" she said.

Katie paused as though she heard the pain in her voice. "Don't worry. Every thing will be all right," she said. "Now tell me where you are and I will be there in a few minutes. The mall is not that far from the house."

The patron sitting a few seats away from Daisy glared at her, frowning. Daisy ignored the man as she continued talking over the phone. She did not realize that she had been loud on the phone.

There was a loud scream as a killer pursued a red haired girl on the big screen.

"What's that?" Katie asked.

"I'm watching a movie," she said.

"Without me?"

Daisy wanted to laugh out loud. "Of course my life has to go on without you," she said.

"Fine," Katie said abruptly. "Don't go. I will be there in a few."

Then without even saying goodbye, she hang up on her.

***

Katie had gained some weight but she still fashioned the beauty of a lady. Daisy had to admit that she missed her.

"I have a plan," Katie said.

"The plan?" Daisy asked.

"Yes," Katie said before becoming silent. She was looking away from her and Daisy wondered if Katie wished she were somewhere else. Then she looked at Daisy. "I missed you. "

Daisy scoffed before chortling.

"It is true," Katie said.

"It doesn't matter." Daisy felt like she meant it, that it didn't matter any longer. She had Freddie.

But lately Freddie changed and Daisy was not sure anymore about their life together.

"Do you love him?" Katie asked. And it was Daisy who felt the immense longing for something wonderful again. The kind that made her feel like she didn't need anything else, which she hardly felt towards her husband.

Daisy didn't answer. Instead, she just stared into Katie's eyes. It was Katie who broke the stare.

CHAPTER 5

Dominic is almost a year old now and Katie was busy with the preparations. It wasn't exactly the celebration she was excited about, but rather the culmination of a plan.

She went inside her room and took her journal. Today— it was simply marked on her calendar.

She checked her figure in the mirror and was happy to find that her stomach had already lost all the ugly lines and fats. A year of dieting did that.

She went outside and was greeted with the ruckus of guests. Everyone was simply Freddie's or her colleagues.

Dominic was carried by Daisy, who looked beautiful in her beige dress. She did look like she was worrying about a lot of things— and Katie's heart went out to her friend. If everything worked out fine today, then... She didn't want to think about the future and hope for a lot. What's important is that she had a plan.

Freddie was talking to some of his colleagues. The tall man was smiling and making some gestures with his hands. He looked like he was a made man, that he had everything he needed. The birthday celebration for Dominic was the irony of a perfect family, where the father, the mother, and the child were there— but they were broken.

"Freddie," Katie said as she walked over to her ex-husband.

Freddie glanced at her and his smile widened. He opened his arms to embrace her warmly.

"Are we waiting for someone else?" He asked.

"Everyone's already here," Katie said.

"Than let's start," Freddie said. He took her hand and walked to the middle of the lawn where a table had been setup. Gifts were piled up on the table, wrapped in mostly blue wrappers.

Freddie raised his right hand while his other was holding Katie's. Katie blushed as she saw Daisy looking at her.

"Dear friends," Freddie started, "thank you for joining us on this wonderful event. I know you're all busy that's why your presence is even more appreciated."

He turned to look at Katie. "Let's all welcome Dominic as he celebrates his birthday."

Everybody turned their heads to look for Dominic, until their eyes settled on Daisy. By this time, Daisy was blushing furiously. She walked to the center of the lawn and stopped beside Freddie.

"How wonderful to have my wife deliver my son," Freddie said before laughing. Everybody who knew that Katie was the mom laughed at Freddie's joke— everybody but the two women.

Katie said, "please everyone, come closer so we can all sing happy birthday to Dominic. She was already holding Dominic.

The guests acceded to her request and in under a minute, everyone was singing. At the end of the song, Katie, who was still holding Dominic, bent forward to blow out the candle. She paused before blowing though, to make a wish— a wish that somehow, her plans would be executed perfectly.

***

In the evening, guests had left and it was only Freddie and Daisy who were still with Katie. Daisy was gathering her things. She fished her car keys and looked at Freddie, "I'm leaving," she said.

"Okay," he said. "Let's go." Freddie turned to Katie and gave Dominic to her.

Now's the time, Katie thought.

"Stay," she said. "Please. At least help me clean up." She flashed her soulful eyes at him, and all but literally begged him to stay.

Freddie turned to look at Daisy, who looked frustrated. "Fine," Daisy said. "Stay all you want." Then without warning, she left.

An icy silence followed.

"I'm sorry about that," Freddie murmured. "You have to understand that she could be jealous of you—"

"It's not a problem," Katie said. "I know she must be."

"Our situation is difficult," Freddie said, pointing out the obvious. "You're her best friend, and you're my ex-wife who had a child with me. I think jealousy is quite the emotion I wish her to have, otherwise I would doubt if she ever has feelings for me."

Katie laughed. "It's difficult—"

"I know. It is. But we're making this work," Freddie said. "I will make it up to her when I get home tonight."

"If you will go home tonight," Katie said.

Freddie's eyes studied Katie. "What do you mean?" he asked,

confused. Katie was holding a sleeping Dominic. She didn't answer Freddie, and instead, walked all the way to Dominic's room. She was putting the boy in his crib when Freddie walked in.

Katie walked over to the doorway where Freddie was standing, staring at her. She turned the lights off.

"What do you mean with what you said? of course I will go home tonight," he said.

Instead of answering him, Katie kissed Freddie.

Freddie's eyes rounded, but how she missed Katie's body. For a split second, he was wondering if what he was doing was right, but when he felt Katie's soft breasts pressing against his chest, all sane thoughts left him, and his hands went automatically to cup her breasts, as though they belonged there. As though his hands were now coming home.

Katie moaned as he kissed her, and it only drove Freddie's arousal to its peak. He carried Katie and brought her to bed, and in a minute, he had unzipped his pants. Katie was already naked, waiting for him in bed.

Before he entered her, Katie pushed him.

"Use protection," she said.

Freddie's eyes tightened. "Why?" he asked.

"I don't want to get pregnant," she said. "What will Daisy say?"

As though in understanding, Freddie obliged. He stood up and rummaged for a condom in his wallet. When he had put it on, he went back to Katie. He was panting as he came quickly.

He rolled on his back, smiling. God, how he missed her.

He was surprised when Katie rolled over and knelt between his thighs. Then carefully, she took off his condom.

"What are you doing?" he asked sleepily.

"Taking care of you," she said. Then she kissed him on his forehead and walked out of the room carrying the used condom.

Inside the bathroom, Katie removed the contents of the condom, put it inside a glass cylinder and cooled it. She will bring it to the sperm bank.

When she went outside the bathroom, Freddie was snoring softly.

CHAPTER 6

It was dawn when Freddie left. Katie had been aware when he stood up and dressed, opened the door of her room and walked out. The the revving of an engine followed as Freddie left to go home to his wife. Katie didn't know what he would tell Daisy, why he arrived home late, but she didn't want to think about what they would discuss about. The important thing was, she had executed her plan.

She stood up and walked over to a desk inside her room. She turned on her laptop, and browsed for a vacation spot. It wouldn't be in Canada where she should book a vacation. She checked sites where there were resorts far from the city. Finally, she saw one that was quite what she wanted. A white beach resort in some far flung area, with an island, and a hill to trek. Perfect. Just what she needed.

Without thinking, she booked three guests. She stood up and took a cigarette while waiting for the confirmation call.

She was anxious about her plan, but if all went well, by the end of next week, she could be starting on with her life.

What would Daisy tell her? She had been in the dark about her plans. What if the plan that they had years ago was no longer remembered by Daisy? What if she was the only one now hoping for this plan to manifest?

She shook her head as though to clear her thoughts.

She blew out cigarette smoke and shivered. She was also afraid. What if there were repercussions? Could she handle them? But everything had been going well, and she didn't think that she could still slip in the execution of her plans.

When her stick had grown shorter, she stubbed the cigarette and went back to her room from the veranda. She stared at the bright screen of her monitor where there in her inbox, the confirmation mail of her booking had just arrived.

She grabbed her mobile phone and called Freddie.

When he picked up, she said, "We're going on a vacation."

She sensed Freddie protesting, so she quickly added, "with Daisy."

With that, Freddie said yes.

***

Waiting was not a fun activity, Katie thought, as she counted the days before the vacation came. She opened an email that Freddie had forwarded to her a long time ago.

His insurance policy stared her in the face.

Then she closed the mail and opened a more recent email from him. It was Daisy's insurance.

Katie smiled to herself as she went to bed that night.

Three more days, she counted inside her head. Everything would go as planned.

***

The day before the vacation, Katie decided to meet with Freddie. She invited him over and as soon as he came in, she grabbed his head and kissed his lips.

By this time, Freddie was no longer confused about the situation. He thought that evidently, Katie wanted him— or at least his body. He was more than willing to allow her to be his mistress.

When they both came, Katie took of his condom again.

"Why do you keep on taking it off me?" he asked, curious.

"So you won't have to wash your hands. I have to pee, so I can do it for you— throw it away in the bin," Katie replied.

Freddie didn't know that inside the bathroom, another glass cylinder awaited his sperm, ready to be delivered to a sperm bank in a few minutes.

He was in bed when the doorbell rang, and without his knowledge, a part of him was being preserved in a sperm bank.

***

Freddie checked his watch. He had stayed with Katie for more than an hour and he was beginning to get antsy. Daisy would definitely ask him where he went and he didn't know what alibi he would give her this time.

He checked his watch again as he was seated on a chair in the dining area.

Katie came in holding two cups of coffee. She put one down in front of Freddie. He smiled at her for the gesture. Immediately, he brought the cup to his lips, whiffed in the glorious scent of coffee and smiled warmly as the taste of the coffee coated his tongue.

"You still make the best coffee," he said.

Katie beamed. She was also drinking her coffee.

"Do you remember our plan before?" she started.

"No—"

"Why you married Daisy? Why we had the divorce?"

Freddie tensed. "That's all in the past now. I'm not divorcing Daisy. What would people say if I get two divorces?"

"We will go on vacation. It is the perfect spot."

Freddie flushed bright red. "What are you talking about?"

"It's all about the money, Freddie," Katie said.

Freddie shook his head. "I don't know what you're talking about—" he said.

"Yes you do! We are in this together," she said. "We divorced so you can be with Daisy— for the money!"

Freddie stood up, shaking his head. "You're crazy."

"I am not. You are the one who's delusional. Don't you remember? We divorced so we could have Daisy's money too," she said.

"She doesn't." Freddie glanced at Katie. "She doesn't have a penny to her name."

Katie looked at him warily. "You're only saying that because you want to back out on what we agreed before. Remember? The two of you will get married, but at the end of it all, you will divorce her to be with me. Then we can have her money too, which is a lot—"

"Was a lot," Freddie highlighted, putting emphasis on was.

Katie froze. "On this vacation, the two of you will fight. Stage it. You can do that for sure. Or sleep with me with her next in the other room. That will surely make her fume. Enough to make her file for divorce, which when that happens, will mean that her assets will be partly yours— and mine too."

"Is this really just about the money for you? Don't you care about your friend?" Freddie yelled.

"Money talks. Money is the only medium we'll ever have that will define our status. Don't play games with me. You will divorce her," Katie said.

Freddie's hand was shaking as he put the coffee down on the table. When he spoke, he was glaring at Katie. "And what if I don't?"

"Then you will have no son to go back to," Katie said.

Freddie's shoulders tensed as he straightened up. His jaw was firm, and his knuckles were white. Then as though in defeat he slowly retreated away from her.

"You're crazy," he said, shaking his head.

Then he turned and walked away. The sound of the door

slamming loudly almost deafened Katie.

She was smiling though. The seed had been planted.

CHAPTER 7

Katie's palms were sweating as she waited at the airport for Freddie and Daisy to come. She left Dominic with a nanny for three days, but if things go according to her plan, she would be able to come home in two days.

It would be dangerous to call Freddie now, to ensure that he had agreed to her plans because she was certain that he was with Daisy now. Better to wait for them to arrive, and then talk to him privately later, or at the latest tomorrow.

She was smoking her second stick when two figures entered the smoking bar at the airport.

Freddie looked like he didn't get to sleep at all. Daisy had lost weight. It seemed as though it was only Katie who had been faring well.

"Hi," she said as she hugged Daisy, and then Freddie.

"Sorry we're late. Traffic," Daisy said.

"No. That's okay. There are no announcements yet about boarding," Katie said.

Freddie sat in the bar and requested a beer, leaving Katie alone with Daisy.

"How are you?" Katie asked.

Daisy raised her eyebrows. "Hell—"

Katie quickly grasped Daisy's hand and gave it a sharp squeeze. "Everything will be all right," she said.
"Make me believe you," Daisy said. "All these years, i've lingered waiting for the chance.. For the plan to unveil. And yet," she stopped, shaking her head. Daisy regarded Katie with a disdainful look before moving away from her to sit beside Freddie.

Katie watched as Freddie took a gulp from his beer. He was probably as anxious as she. Katie wondered if Daisy would be forgiving once she learned all about her plans. She had to go with her.
The preparations were all according to plan, and Katie could

not wait to unleash them.

Katie remembered her conversation with Freddie the other day.

***

"Come on," Katie said. "I know that we haven't talked about it in a long time... but just think about it, all the money—nobody would have to work anymore," Katie said.

Freddie was drunk. "I know that I haven't fallen for Daisy the way I did with you, but she's my wife now, and I don't think I can hurt her."

"Just go with me on the vacation," she said. "I will handle everything."

"What's the plan?" he asked.

"Three will go to the island," Katie said, pausing, "but only two will come back."

Freddie's face blanched. "Surely you don't mean to kill her—"

Katie's lips thinned as she smiled. "Of course I won't kill her."

"Promise me," Freddie asked.

"I promise," Katie has said. She had meant to keep the promise too. "But you have to do your part. Ask for the divorce, and leave everything else to me."

Freddie nodded reluctantly. "Hell, what are we going to do with the money? Why do you need so much?"

At that, Katie slapped Freddie. "Think about Dominic. Think about your son. He needs to have a good future."

"I have money— and you can always go back to work so you can shoulder some of the boy's expenses," he said.

"I don't need pennies. Listen, if you're not up for it, then just tell me," Katie said.

Freddie's eyes softened. Katie had known that if she said those exact words, she would be able to convince Freddie.

He nodded slightly. "We'll do this together. Just the divorce. Then we split the assets. From there, I don't know—"

"Don't worry," Katie said. "When all this is over, you won't have to worry about anything anymore."

***

As Freddie gulped on his beer, he was remembering his conversation with Katie the other day. She had told him that when everything was over, he would have no worries anymore. He just wished that it could be now. How he longed to have this trip over.

He felt sorry for Daisy. Katie had been clear that only two would return from the trip and no matter how much Freddie justified in his head the act that he would commit, he still felt a bitter taste in his mouth.

It's all for the money, he told himself.

He had doubts though about Daisy's money— which was something he found difficult to understand. Katie was certain that Daisy had money and yet, the way his wife had been acting didn't lead him into believing that she actually had any.

At this point, Freddie found it irrelevant. Once Daisy had been taken care of, he would be the lone beneficiary to her insurance.

Maybe, just maybe, Katie and her plans to dispose of Daisy was actually a good move.

CHAPTER 8

Katie had nothing on her mind when the plane landed, and the three of them boarded a cruise ship. The deck was only spacious enough to hold a handful of people, so she got up and walked over before the place becomes bustling with the crowd.

An attendant smiled at her and offered her a cocktail, which she accepted graciously.

"Thank you," she said, smiling although she didn't feel like it.

The attendant smiled back at her and left.

To her front lay the sparse sea. The island could not be viewed yet. As indicated in the itinerary, the sail would take around an hour, which meant enough time for her to clear her thoughts and think about the plan that she laid down. She didn't want any loopholes.

The wind was blowing hard, and it hit her in the face so she took out her sunglasses from her purse and put them on. She lit a cigarette while she studied the waters.

"Penny for your thoughts," Daisy said from behind her.

Katie turned to her friend.

"This is the plan," she said.

Daisy looked confused. "What are you talking about?" she asked.

"After this vacation, everything will be back to normal. No more hiding, no more pretenses— just everything that we ever dreamed of when we were young," Katie said.

"I don't know what you're talking about—"

"Of course you do! You were with me when we were planning this years ago, weren't you? Marry a man! Get a child! Loot him for his money—" Katie paused. Her voice had gone loud. She was thankful for the wind that was coating her voice. "Weren't those our plans? So we could finally be together? Wasn't that what we talked about? To retaliate against the world for discriminating against us?" Katie was already yelling.

Daisy flinched. "You keep on confusing me," she said. "I didn't really mean it that way—"

"But say you're not bailing out on me!" Katie insisted. "Tell me we will do this together."

"Calm down," Daisy said.

"I will not calm down!" Katie said. "I spent the past years of my life to see this plan into fruition. It will happen, Daisy, with or without your help!"

Daisy stared at her friend. Katie's eyes were red as though from lack of sleep. Clearly, she had been sleeping less.

"Let's go back inside—" Daisy started.

"No, leave me here," Katie said.

When Katie didn't budge from where she was standing, Daisy decided to stay beside her. She watched the waves with her friend.

"Do you remember how we used to love the beach?" Daisy asked.

Katie nodded, then drank her cocktail.

"We were in college then and we would skip classes just to take a two hour drive to the nearest resort," Daisy said. After a while, she added, "We were different then than we are now." She glanced at Katie. "I'd like to think that the difference between *the us* before and *the us* we had become is that we are more mature now."
"I miss you so much, Daisy," Katie said.

Daisy didn't say anything as though she was thinking hard. "I miss you so much too," she said. With that she turned to leave.

Minutes passed after Daisy left, and Katie still stood there on the deck, lost in her thoughts, vehemently planning her next steps. Then she threw the glass she was holding on the railing, making it shatter upon impact.

"Shit!" she cursed. "All of this for nothing?" she whispered to herself. "I will not be defeated. I will have this plan executed. At the end of the vacation, two would return, and it would have to be Daisy and me," she said quietly to herself. Her eyes had lost their focus as though lunacy fled her temporarily.

CHAPTER 9

The first night on the island was riddled with half-hearted conversations. Mostly, it was Daisy who did the talking.

"Where are we off to tomorrow?" she asked.

"I have everything planned out," Katie said. "I hired a boat."

Freddie glanced at her. He frowned. "How big is the boat?"

"Enough for the three of us," she said.

"I don't think I want to go tomorrow," he said. "I will just stay here. The two of you can go and catch up."

Katie's eyes narrowed. "You will go with us."

"Not if I don't want to," Freddie said.

"I think I will leave you two alone for now," Daisy cut in, "so that whatever disagreements the two of you have, you can settle it. I don't want to be caught in the middle." Then she stood up and headed back to the room, leaving Freddie and Katie alone by the beach front.

As Freddie watched Daisy go away, he wondered why he had not paid attention to her more keenly. It seemed like he was married to the right woman. Sure, she had some flaws, but no one is perfect.

"So why won't you go boating with us?" Katie said.

Freddie shrugged. He felt leaden inside. The past days had kept him wide awake at night just thinking about the divorce that Katie was nagging him about.

"I don't want to divorce Daisy," he said.

Katie's eyes rounded. "You bastard! Freddie, listen to me. We have gotten far enough. If not the divorce, then we have to silence her one way or another."

"I am not the bastard here," he said.

44

"This is the plan. Why are you not being true to your word?" Katie shouted.

"It is some sick game you want to play," Freddie said. "Look, I've been thinking about this. Maybe it isn't right anymore to keep seeing each other. It's not healthy for you. And it's making me suffer too. Dominic— well, I can always visit him from time to time. Don't worry about child support, I won't stop providing for my son."

"This is not how we planned it!" Katie shouted. "You're not supposed to turn tables around. Don't you remember it is me you love."

"Was," Freddie said. "It was you. But now, it *is* Daisy I love."

Katie's eyes filled with tears and in frustration, she scratched at her face and tore her hair alternately. Her eyes clouded as though lost. Freddie just watched her.

"Listen," Freddie said. "Find a good man. With your looks, I'm sure you'll find many. I used to love you, but the moment you asked me to divorce Daisy made me think. You were not the person I fell in love with anymore."

"Please— just please go with us tomorrow," Katie pleaded. "I won't insist anymore on the divorce. Just please go."

Freddie watched as a steady stream of tears welled from Katie's eyes. He thought that she at least deserved this last request, so he said yes.

***

At twelve midnight, Katie was wide awake. She had to convince Freddie to go with them boating. It was the only way she could execute her plans.

When five in the morning struck, Katie had not slept at all. Not even one wink. She dressed up, ready for the boat. Plans had changed. Maybe it was her fault, scheming behind the two married people.

But she would push through with the plan.

She clutched at her purse as she waited for the clock to strike exactly five thirty. Then she would head down and meet Daisy and Freddie by the dock. Today— whatever happens, two will return to the island. Only two, she kept telling herself.

It was kind of last minute arrangement, but she was thankful when Daisy called her up and told her she had changed her mind. "The car," Daisy had said, "had been taken care of."

Katie went down and started for the dock.

The breeze was chilly and goose bumps riddled her arms. She was oblivious to the cold air as she walked down to the dock. When she arrived, Freddie and Daisy were nowhere to be seen so she sat down waiting. She opened her purse and stared at the knife stowed inside. The blade glittered under the moonlight.

Only two would come back, she kept telling herself.

***

At six in the morning, all three of them were already on the boat.

Freddie had taken the wheel and they were now cruising.

Katie felt alone as she watched Freddie steer the wheel. Daisy was sitting on a chair beside where Freddie was. They were having a conversation.

Freddie turned to look at Daisy who smiled at him in return.

At that moment, a surge of jealousy sprouted from Katie's heart and she couldn't take it anymore. The beautiful picture in front of her used to be hers. It should be like it was before. Daisy hers.

Without thinking, she took out the knife and stealthily walked towards the two. She was gripping the knife with both hands.

Only a yard away, she thought. Then she raised her right hand and plunged the knife against Freddie's body.

Freddie was caught in surprise. Daisy yelled and grabbed Freddie who had fallen down.

Katie kept on attacking with her knife, but her next thrusts didn't land on Freddie's body anymore as the latter kicked her, sending her sprawling to the ground.

"You think that this is fun?" Katie said. "You took everything from me!"

"Stop it," Daisy said. "It's not meant to be. You have changed. You are no longer the woman I fell in love with."

"Why?" Katie said. "Do you think you can make me believe that you have become straight?" Katie laughed maniacally, her eyes dancing as they went wild.

"The plans— they were nothing. Just spur of the moment thing. It wasn't my fault that you held on to those plans!"

"But the phone calls!" Katie said. "You always call me and beg me to take you back when I was still married to Freddie."

"Move on," Daisy said. "Everything changes."

"Shit!" Katie said. She was standing again, walking towards them, hand thrust out, ready to attack.

"Please don't do this—" Daisy begged. "Freddie is bleeding. We have to take him back to the island."

"I don't care! He is a traitor just like you!"

"You're crazy!" Freddie yelled. Then to Daisy he said, "she wanted me to divorce you."

"You wanted to when you were thrusting into me!" Katie said, before laughing loudly.

Daisy looked pained.

"Yes. Your husband slept with me," Katie said. When the pain didn't leave Daisy's eyes, she said, "Don't be mad at me! Be mad at Freddie. I only did it because of our plans. See, I stole his sperm. It's in a sperm bank. We can have another baby anytime we want. Just like we planned."

Daisy's eyes shone with unshed tears. She looked at Freddie, "Is that true?"

"I am sorry," he said.

Those words unleashed the anger inside Daisy. She stood up and walked away from Freddie. Her eyes never left Katie.

"You're right," Daisy said. "He's easy to tempt. We shouldn't be together. I should go back to you."

Katie smiled widely. "That's what I've been telling you. He has insurance. We'll be millionaires when all this is over. Two would come back to the island. We'll report drowning—"

"Hush," Daisy said. "Don't tell him what we would do. Let his cheating body bleed to death—"

Daisy was now an arm's length away from Katie. "Let him bleed to death," she said one more time before jumping at Katie. Katie, who was taken by surprise struggled against Daisy. But Daisy was stronger. She tried to take the knife away, but Katie held on to it with a vise grip.

When she realized what was happening, Katie tried to attack Daisy with the knife, but Daisy was strong and her hand won't budge from the grip. Katie looked around for support, for anything to throw Daisy off. She kicked at the table near them, sending it atop Daisy who yelped as the edge hit her back.

Katie stood up and ran towards Freddie. "When you are dead, Daisy would come back to me," she said crazily.

Then she jumped at him and raised her hand, ready to strike again, but before the knife touched Freddie's body, Daisy had hit her with a chair. Katie collapsed unconsciously on top of Freddie.

Daisy was shaking. "Is she dead?" she asked.

"I don't know," Freddie said. "I hope she is though." He was holding his wound.

"Did you mean that—? Bleed me to death?" he asked.

Daisy who was still shaking shook her head vehemently. "No— I never realized before that I didn't want to lose you until now. Until last night actually. Katie thought to hurt you. And I couldn't just let it happen. It was pretense, so I could get close enough to attack her..."

She stopped talking as Katie stirred and raised her hand up, taking the knife and plunging it against Daisy's stomach.

2

It was too late. Freddie had not prevented the attack. He got up and kicked at Katie, took the knife from her with one blow. He stabbed Katie once, then he raised his hand again to keep stabbing Katie.

"No!" Daisy shouted. "That's enough. Don't kill her. It's not worth it."

"She wants to kill us," Freddie said.

"Not anymore when she's unconscious," Daisy pointed out.

Freddie stood up, staggering. His wound was bleeding badly.

"We have a life ahead of us. We'll take Dominic. I don't want you to rot in jail," Daisy said.

Freddie winced as pain clutched at his wound.

"Go. Take us back to the shore. I will handle Katie. I will turn her over to security, and then run as fast as you can. Take the car to the nearest station. Be fast and report everything to the authorities," Daisy said. "Everything will be all right. Nobody has to die."

Freddie nodded. He walked towards the wheel and steered it back towards the dock. He was shaking as he had lost a fair amount of blood. But he would make it to the docks. He would do as Daisy had said. And before the day was over, everything would have turned out right.

***

The boat lurched as Freddie worked on stopping it. The boat hit the ledge, but he didn't care anymore. All he wanted was to jump off the boat and straight into the car, drive as fast as he could and tell everything to the authorities.

"Go now," Daisy said urgently at him.

Katie was still lying on the floor. Daisy had wrapped a bandage on Katie's wound and the bleeding had seemed to stop.

Daisy stood up and hugged him tightly. "Go now," she urged again.

Without another word, Freddie turned around and left the boat. Pain lacerated all over his body but he was oblivious to it anymore. He all but dragged his legs. He saw the rented car, and took out the car keys. The door opened and slammed so quickly before Freddie had taken his seat. In a rush, he didn't bother anymore with the seatbelt.

As soon as the engine was turned on, Freddie hit the gas pedal. The car took off with the weight of his foot.

Freddie's heart was racing as he fought to stay conscious throughout the drive. He looked at the rear-view mirror and saw that the boat was still there. He wished that Daisy had Katie under control. How he prayed that his ex-wife would remain unconscious until he had reported everything. In a few minutes, the police would surround the boat, and Daisy would be taken to the hospital to be healed for her wounds.

When he glanced at the rear-view mirror again, two figures were emerging from the boat.

He looked back, confused and saw Daisy with Katie, walking out of the boat and into the ledge.

Freddie's mouth hung open as he worried that Katie would start on a rage again and kill Daisy. But what Katie did was hold Daisy's waist as Daisy supported a limping Katie.

Freddie wanted to turn around and go back and kill Katie so he pressed the gas pedal to the floor and maneuvered a U-turn. But the car jerked forward so he hit the brakes. To his surprise, the brakes didn't work. Instead, the car continued careening towards the edge of the road.

Freddie's hands rammed frantically at the wheel to get the car back on the road. He breathed a sigh of relief as he avoided hitting a tree. He was back on the road again.

Who the hell messed up with the brakes? he wondered.

It seemed like the only way to go about this day was to head on to the police. Forget Daisy's safety for the meantime—he told himself. So he gassed up again and the car jerked again as it engaged speed.

He wasn't aware that there was a sharp curve ahead, and when it was within a good five yards, Freddie yelped as he turned the steering wheel 360 degrees to avoid flying towards the vast sea.

The car swerved sharply to the right and Freddie urged for the car to stop by hitting the brakes. But no matter how hard he pressed the brakes, it didn't work. He fought with the wheel as though it had its own life. But as soon as he was back on the road, a dog emerged from the bushes. It was a dark brown husky, and he couldn't run over it so he steered the wheel frantically, until he lost sense of direction and the car raced full speed out into the sea.

The car landed on the water and started to sink. Freddie forced the door open but it wouldn't budge. He rolled the windows down desperately until water started pouring from the window. The car was sinking fast.

Freddie swam, but before he could get out of the window, his jeans snagged on the car seat and he couldn't get out.

"Shit!" He muttered. He waved frantically as the car slowly pulled him down into the bottom of the sea.

As Freddie started to drown, that was when realization hit him—he had been prey to the two women. All they wanted was his insurance money. And with him gone, he wondered what sick excuse they would have over his death.

He was taken by the waters in five minutes. With that, he breathed his last.

CHAPTER 10

Katie clutched tightly at Daisy's hand as she walked towards the ambulance. All around her, nurses and paramedics milled busily, checking on her and Daisy.

Several paramedics helped her to lie down on the stretcher. Daisy, who was less injured, only allowed for bandage to be wrapped around her and insisted on riding with Katie.

A tall, bald police officer approached Katie.

"Ms Hamilton, I need to get some statements," he said. He was holding a paper and pen.

"I need to know if we are safe first," Katie said. "What happened to Freddie?" She asked.
The police officer stared blankly at her before speaking. "His body was found drowned thirty minutes ago. He was rushed to the hospital, but he was pronounced dead on arrival."

A sob escaped Daisy's lips. "He is—was my husband," she said.

"I'm getting confused," the officer said as he narrowed his eyes.

"I'm his ex-wife," Katie said. "We have a baby together, but Daisy is his wife now."

"And you are friends?" he said.

"Yes," Katie said.

"How did he die?" Daisy asked.

"His car flew off the road and straight into the sea. No investigations yet, but we will be looking if the engine has been tampered with," the officer replied.

"But for now we are safe?" Katie said.

The officer nodded. "Now, tell me what happened."

Katie exchanged a glance Daisy before speaking.

"We went boating. I never suspected it, but right when we were in the middle of the sea, Freddie lost his temper and started attacking us. He wanted both of us dead. He only turned back to the docks when I managed to stab him," Katie said. "He was probably scared of his wound that's why he turned around and hurried away," she paused, shaking her head sadly, "only to save himself."

"But what would be his motive?" The officer asked. His brows were furrowed.

It was Daisy who replied. "Insurance money probably."

"We're getting that a lot," the officer said. "But we have to look deeper into this. The records say that he had money to his name too."

"He could never get enough," Katie said.

"What a sad man," the officer said, sighing.

The paramedics approached them. "Officer, we need to take them now. I believe the questioning can continue at a later time," a blonde woman said.

The officer retreated reluctantly. "By all means," he said. Then to Katie and Daisy he added, "Miss Hamilton, I will be in touch."

The paramedic closed the ambulance door, and in a few seconds, the van was already moving. The sirens filled the air.

Daisy leaned over to Katie and kissed her forehead.

"I never knew we would come to this," she said in a soft voice. "We planned it a long time ago, and now, everything is going to be fine—just the two of us—finally."

"You scared me," Katie said. "Back there in the boat, you fought me, and I thought you really meant to kill me."

"That was all part of the act so I could urge Freddie into driving the car," Daisy said. "I had to make him believe that his interest was what I had in mind. If he had suspected, he would have killed us both."

Katie smiled and nodded in understanding. "We have Dominic now all to ourselves plus the insurance money from Freddie's death."

Daisy nodded. "I feel sorry for him. He was a kind man."

"Yes, he gave us everything. We owe our happiness to him," Katie agreed. "But we had to do this."

Daisy smiled wanly. "I know. The best part is that we still have his sperm in a bank and we could get you pregnant anytime again—once you are well."

"And this time, you will be there every step of the way, just like we dreamed," Katie said.

Daisy pressed a kiss against Katie's lips lightly. "I love you. I can't wait to live my every day with you," Daisy said.

"I have been waiting for this for so long," Katie said. "Now we have us. Now we start the journey."

Daisy smiled broadly this time as she squeezed Katie's hand tightly. "To us."

As the ambulance skirted along the road, the red and blue lights danced as though instead of declaring urgency, they were announcing to the world a celebration of a joyous union.

Indeed, three had come to the sea, and only two came back.

The End

ABOUT THE AUTHOR

Richard J. Garcia

Richard J. Garcia is an American writer, born in Maryland in 1971.

He has been working with writing challenged clients for over six years. He provides ghost writing, coaching and ghost editing services. His educational background in family science and journalism has given him a broad base from which to approach many topics.

Richard J. Garcia became a full-time writer. He spent many years in different parts of the World to inspire his imaginations. He now lives in Koh Samui, Thailand.

Printed in Great Britain
by Amazon

46563502R00040